"Everyone who knows a dog well knows one thing: dogs live for the precious moments when they can interact with humans and when they can play. They're an absolute pleasure and this wonderful little book captures it perfectly. It's a real treat for young and old."

—David Liddle, PhD,
inventor and entrepreneur

"This book tells the story of what some jubilant canine cousins would have written to please their cherished and loyal people. The book begs to be read to kids lucky enough to have their own puppy to train, love and admire."

—Meg Withgott, PhD,
Entrepreneur

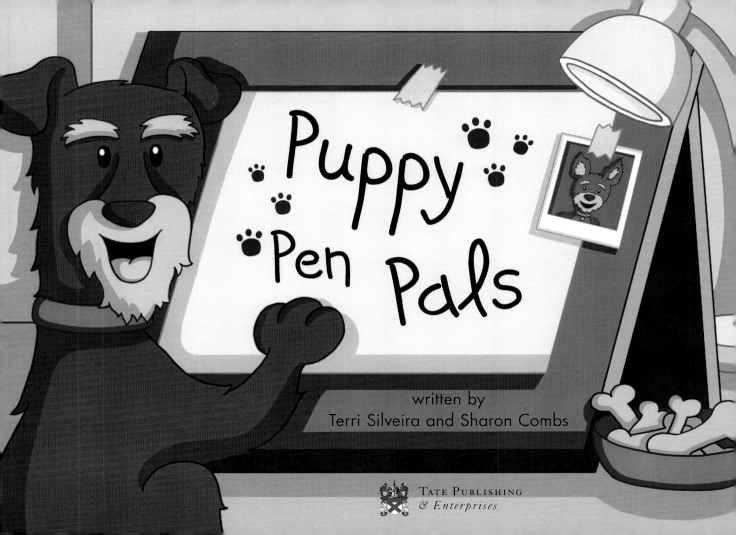

Published by Tate Publishing & Enterprises, LLC
127 E. Trade Center Terrace | Mustang, Oklahoma 73064 USA
1.888.361.9473 | www.tatepublishing.com

Tate Publishing is committed to excellence in the publishing industry. The company reflects the philosophy established by the founders, based on Psalm 68:11,
*"The Lord gave the word and great was the company of those who published it."*

Book design copyright © 2009 by Tate Publishing, LLC. All rights reserved.
*Cover and Interior design by Eddie Russell*
*Illustration by Kathy Hoyt*

Published in the United States of America

ISBN: 978-1-60799-454-1
1. Juvenile Fiction: Animals: Dogs
2. Juvenile Fiction: Animals: Pets
09.06.22

This book is dedicated to our beloved

Samson and Max

Dear Samson,

I just wanted to introduce myself to you; I'm Max, your one-and-a-half-year-old cousin! I live in a great house with a wonderful family that takes really good care of me. They always feed me on time and never give me table scraps, even though I sometimes want them. They take me outside when they think I need to go potty and sometimes I have to go bad! My family always makes sure I know what I can do and what I'm not supposed to do.

I'm a lucky dog, I got to go with my family to the mountains, where I met your new family. They are really nice, especially the little girl, Kelly. You two will have lots of fun times together, and I bet she'll take you for walks.

I hope to meet you soon so we can play together. Good luck in your new home and welcome to the family, kid.

Your Older Cousin,
Max

Dear Max,

Thank you for your letter and picture; you're one good-looking dude. My dad just picked these pictures up last night; I'm pretty cute and adorable, aren't I? I'm really enjoying my new home. My dad's more strict than my mom and Kelly, but they're starting to say "No" like he does, especially when I bite. Kelly says, "No bite, no bite!" I don't mean to bite hard, but sometimes I get a little rambunctious when we play.

Yesterday Mom and Kelly took me to the doctor. It was my first time, and it wasn't very fun. The nurse had to take my temperature, and the doctor had to look in my ears and give me a shot. But Kelly was right beside me with lots of love and hugs, telling me what a good, brave puppy I was. When it was all over, the doctor gave me a cookie and said I'm a healthy eight-week-old, three-pound puppy.

When you were little, did you like to chew on shoelaces? Mom and Dad don't like it when I chew on their shoelaces, so they buy me toys to chew on instead. I've got some balls and squeaky toys that Kelly and I play with together. We also play a game called Chase Me, Chase Me in the backyard, where she runs after me then I run after her. It makes me bark and her giggle. After all our playing I get hungry, and Kelly feeds me three times a day.

Well, I'm a little tired after playing and eating; I think it's time for a nap. I hope we can meet someday; I'd like to play with you too.

Bye Max,

Your Cousin Sam

Dear Sam,

Yes, you are cute and adorable, and someday you'll be as handsome as me.

My family brushes me at least two times a week and sometimes it hurts (just a little). They try to be gentle so I really don't mind, especially when they finish because then everyone tells me how handsome I am and I get lots of hugs.

Have they started giving you baths? That is not my idea of fun, but I sure smell good afterward. So take my advice, cousin, and just stand real still, and it's over before you know it.

You asked me if I chew on shoelaces, well I kind of do, but only to tease my mom so she'll chase me. For exercise I get to go running almost every day. When I see the funny shoes and heavy socks being put on I know it's time. I get so excited I run to the door and wait for my leash because we have a leash law. No dogs on public streets without a leash, and we always follow the rules. We see other dogs on our outings, and they bark at me, but some of them wag their tails, so I know they're friendly.

It's time for my dinner! That means I need to get someone's attention. I usually just sit and stare, but if that doesn't work, I jump up and bark very loud. That always works!

Be good, Sam,
Max

Hi Cousin Max,

How's everything with you and your family? I'm doing pretty good, but boy, it's tough being a puppy. My mom and dad have to leave me by myself during the day. The good part is I have my very own room that I stay in when they're gone. I have all my toys in there, lots of fresh water, and my bed. I also have lots of clean newspaper in case I can't wait until they come home to go potty. The newspaper is on the other side of my room, far away from my bed.

I'm put in my room in the morning and I usually just sleep. Then Dad comes home and feeds me lunch, and we play for a little while in the backyard. Then I have to go back in my room. I don't really mind being in my room, though. It's a nice, safe place to be. I can't get into any trouble in my room because it's puppy-proof. There are no electric cords for me to chew on.

I get a little lonely, but Kelly, Mom, and Dad make up for it. We have lots of special times, when we all play together with lots of hugs and love.

Kelly's got this thing about everything being clean, including me. She'll say, "Come on Sam, it's grooming time," and she brushes me every day. As far as baths, yes, I get a bath once a week. Kelly's always careful not to get any water in my ears, and she uses this cool puppy shampoo that doesn't sting my eyes. Then she rinses me really well to make sure all the shampoo's out.

I like the water, but I'm not too sure about this bathing thing. Thanks for the advice about trying to stand still, maybe I'll try it. Sometimes I try to jump out of the water and run away. It never seems to work, though. Kelly always has a good hold on me.

That's great that you get lots of exercise. I have to stay in my own backyard, away from other dogs until I get older and I've had all my shots.

Hey, do you do any tricks? I'm trying to learn to sit. When I do it, I get a cookie, and boy do I love cookies!

Well, it's special time with the family, so I'm going to go play. Do you ever roll over and get your tummy rubbed? My mom always says, "It's good luck to rub a puppy tummy." Plus, I really like it.

Thanks for all the advice. I'm glad we're family and you can help me grow up to be a good dog, like you.

Love from,
Your Cousin Sam

Dear Cousin Max,

Thank you so much for the Christmas present. I call him Froggy. He's my favorite squeaky toy, and I play with him all the time. I got some other really cool Christmas gifts. My mom and dad gave me some peanut butter cookies that I really like. They are shaped like peanuts. I also got a stocking with toys and good things to eat in it. I hope you had a good Christmas too.

Guess what! On February 23, I'll be one year old!

Even though I'm growing up, Kelly says I'll always be her little puppy. I hope I get some more of those peanut butter cookies for my birthday. I know I'm getting bigger, but I think Kelly's growing up too; she looks taller.

You take care, Cousin!

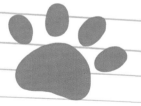

Love,
Cousin Sam

Dear Sam,

What a birthday surprise to meet you finally, along with our families, in the mountains. It was a real treat for the puppy pen pals to play together all day. I'm proud to say you've grown up to be a good, loving companion.

Congratulations on your first birthday, and I hope you and your family have a lifetime full of daily walks, love, and happiness.

Hope to see you again for more playtime,
Cousin Max

# e|LIVE

## listen|imagine|view|experience

### AUDIO BOOK DOWNLOAD INCLUDED WITH THIS BOOK!

In your hands you hold a complete digital entertainment package. Besides purchasing the paper version of this book, this book includes a free download of the audio version of this book. Simply use the code listed below when visiting our website. Once downloaded to your computer, you can listen to the book through your computer's speakers, burn it to an audio CD or save the file to your portable music device (such as Apple's popular iPod) and listen on the go!

How to get your free audio book digital download:

1. Visit www.tatepublishing.com and click on the e|LIVE logo on the home page.
2. Enter the following coupon code:
   8623-d994-489b-302b-4c0f-c900-8e7f-490c
3. Download the audio book from your e|LIVE digital locker and begin enjoying your new digital entertainment package today!